SOMEWHAT ABSURD, SOMEHOW EXISTENTIAL

Poetry

ESSENTIAL POETS SERIES 286

Canada Council   Conseil des Arts
for the Arts   du Canada

ONTARIO ARTS COUNCIL
CONSEIL DES ARTS DE L'ONTARIO

Canadä

Guernica Editions Inc. acknowledges the support of the Canada Council for the
Arts and the Ontario Arts Council. The Ontario Arts Council is an agency of the
Government of Ontario.

We acknowledge the financial support of the Government of Canada.

SOMEWHAT ABSURD, SOMEHOW EXISTENTIAL

Poetry

J. J. Steinfeld

GUERNICA
EDITIONS

TORONTO – CHICAGO – BUFFALO – LANCASTER (U.K.)
2021

Michael Mirolla, editor
Cover and Interior Design: Errol F. Richardson
Cover painting: Brenda Whiteway,
Encroachment (triptych, middle panel, oil on canvas)
Guernica Editions Inc.
287 Templemead Drive, Hamilton (ON), Canada L8W 2W4
2250 Military Road, Tonawanda, N.Y. 14150-6000 U.S.A.
www.guernicaeditions.com

Distributors:
Independent Publishers Group (IPG)
600 North Pulaski Road, Chicago IL 60624
University of Toronto Press Distribution (UTP)
5201 Dufferin Street, Toronto (ON), Canada M3H 5T8
Gazelle Book Services
White Cross Mills, High Town, Lancaster LA1 4XS U.K.

First edition.
Printed in Canada.

Legal Deposit – Third Quarter
Library of Congress Catalog Card Number: 2021933084
Library and Archives Canada Cataloguing in Publication
Title: Somewhat absurd, somehow existential : poetry / J. J. Steinfeld.
Names: Steinfeld, J. J., author.
Series: Essential poets ; 286.
Description: Series statement: Essential poets ; 286
Identifiers: Canadiana 20210140380 | ISBN 9781771836043 (softcover)
Subjects: LCGFT: Poetry.
Classification: LCC PS8587.T355 S66 2021 | DDC C811/.54—dc23

For Lisa Logan and Andrew Frontini,
and for Brenda,
with love somewhat and somehow
beyond the absurd or the existential, as always

BOOKS BY
J. J. STEINFELD ~~~

The Apostate's Tattoo (Stories)
Our Hero in the Cradle of Confederation (Novel)
Forms of Captivity and Escape (Stories)
Unmapped Dreams (Stories)
The Miraculous Hand and Other Stories
Dancing at the Club Holocaust (Stories)
Disturbing Identities (Stories)
Should the Word Hell Be Capitalized? (Stories)
Anton Chekhov Was Never in Charlottetown (Stories)
Would You Hide Me? (Stories)
An Affection for Precipices (Poetry)
Word Burials (Novel and Stories)
Misshapenness (Poetry)
A Glass Shard and Memory (Stories)
Identity Dreams and Memory Sounds (Poetry)
Madhouses in Heaven, Castles in Hell (Stories)
An Unauthorized Biography of Being (Stories)
Absurdity, Woe Is Me, Glory Be (Poetry)
A Visit to the Kafka Café (Poetry)
Gregor Samsa Was Never in The Beatles (Stories)
Morning Bafflement and Timeless Puzzlement (Poetry)
Somewhat Absurd, Somehow Existential (Poetry)

Contents

Caught in Someone Else's Misdirected Film

There must be an exact instant
when day in all its clarity
turns to enigmatic night
when magic praised
turns to ordinariness
hopefulness to unfulfilment
an instant pondered and analyzed
not far removed from the exact moment
when love turns to hate
or memory to forgetfulness
the words from a song
evocative of youth
rearrange into agedness
and sour nostalgia.

There must be a collapsed epiphany
when the perfect phrasing of sense
turns to senselessness
hinged on a misspelling
or painful mispronunciation.

There must be a precise time
when in a long life
understanding and comprehension
turn to a lost recollection
when instants, moments, epiphanies noted
in a secret ledger
its whereabouts known
only to your heart
your timeless lost heart.

These thoughts of being occur as you look
an unexpected stranger in the eye
more like a misplaced or misshapen self
both of you caught in someone else's misdirected film
amidst the confusion and distraction
curiosity suddenly turns to fear
admiration to contempt
one runs away swiftly
the other holds his ground
pretends to be courageous
and timeless.

Aberration

Once, just once,
I want to meet someone
who defies explanation
and eludes description
even lavish adjectives
and no-nonsense nouns
someone a little too tall
or a little too short for the factual
who nudges toward the inexplicable
who would swim in either love
or lovelessness with equal speed
someone outside of exemplary or despised
outside of even outcast or other
someone sidestepping oddness
and circumventing strangeness
someone who the tabloids, the worst tabloids,
would shun
and the holy or erudite
would merely overlook
perhaps cough politely
and at best say
they'd get back to you
after some prayer
and consultation.

Startles You All the Same

Startling, isn't it, sad lost soul,
—I forget your name so I'll
turn you into someone symbolic—
when you realize how simple,
simple as falling off a cliff
after a night of drinking,
to confuse truth with lies
the eternal with the moment
who you are with who you were
but startling is just the start
when you confuse yesterday with today
past love with future hate
madness with clarity
the end of the long line
with the beginning of the line—
oh well, you are standing in line
that is obvious and simple
and the tap on the shoulder
a little softer than last time
startles you all the same.

A New Voice for Incantations

I say the incantation
yet another time
summon nothing
but the reminder
of what is out of reach.

Should I change my clothes
create a captivating disguise
or a surreptitious smile
something to entice
those in charge of
the inexplicable
and incomprehensible?

I change my shadow
redefine my words
and by nightfall
devise a new voice
for incantations.

Louder, a clever lilt,
stand on the most
advantageous side of the moon
silly if not self-defeating
to cease my attempts:
it could be a necessary ghost
it could be a vital soul
the wind might indeed
be something else.

Magical Stories

Sex is magical
the down-on-his-luck magician
says, finding the porn site
the assistant he had cut in half
recommended between acts.

Escape is magical
the down-on-her-luck ballerina
says, taking the magical pills
the partner she had danced with
gave her after a lacklustre performance.

Science is magical
the three down-on-their-luck scientists
say, no one believing their teleporter
would ever work in any way
as they disappear from sight.

God is magical
the down-on-their-luck couple
say, prepared to leap off a cliff
the angel-like wings securely affixed
given them after praying haphazardly.

Life is magical
the down-on-its-luck seagull
thinks, flying above the desperately
wing-flapping couple
now cursing God and magic.

This Looming Captivity

There it was
covering a residential street
a mystery without humour
a size laughing at houses
a shape tricking sense
and I was prepared
to walk around or through it
depending on my negotiations
with fate and destiny.
So much for boldness
and good intentions
I was as motionless
as lifelong failure
and futile predictions
of the end of the world.
What to do to escape
this looming captivity?
Where to run, how to hide?
In the end I leaped over the mystery
and banged my head on the corner
of a quarrelsome quarter moon
hoping I'll simply float back
and resume my evening walk
before the inexplicable
takes an indisputable foothold
in my neighbourhood.

Mortifying Thoughts

Sure is mortifying
when you turn around
and a snarling wraith
sucker punches you.

Sure is mortifying
when you start praying
and you hear laughter
from above.

Sure is mortifying
when you meet God
and are mistaken for a character
who has lost his way.

Sure is mortifying
when you are asked
to spell *mortifying* and you get
two of the letters wrong.

Sure is mortifying
when you meet yourself
and neither one of you
has anything profound to say.

The Approaching Creature

If and when you become invisible
your punishment will be
that you cannot comprehend invisibility
such is the contrariness of the fantastic
in the everyday, the ordinary,
the thin surface of consistency.

Have you seen everything you need to see
or is there still an astonishment
off in the distance
small like the promise of eternity
you want to catch a glimpse of?

You have run out of words
and you cry because you have nothing to say
to stop the approaching creature
larger than any you have previously imagined.

Visitation

A sad voice without a source
a light, intense and abrupt,
without an explanation
makes the woman close the book
she had been reading
because sleep had again been elusive.
Yesterday, not today,
was the anniversary of her husband's death
she thinks, then whispers,
as if that is the source and the explanation
her husband, a day and a year gone,
who had not wanted a funeral
firm in his desire to be cremated
and his ashes spread in the wind.
I want not a trace of me
except in your memory,
he had said, her ear close to his lips,
his words a heartbeat from incomprehension
his body's betrayal sinister and complete.
But she goes to the urn and opens it
to see if he is still there
hoping the sad voice and the intense light
are not angry with her.

A Dream of Dream Lovers

It is a dream of a dream
during which you're sleeping
with the woman of your dreams
and she can read minds
and perform sensual magic
that would make any magician of lust envious
she's attempting to outdo legendary lovers
you think of Cleopatra
you think of Mata Hari
you think of both of them at once
lips more brilliant and historical
than in any forbidden novel of your youth
you add into the amorous mix
a few flappers and *femme fatales*
Billie Holiday is singing
but she's suffered too much
to summon to a dream bed.

The dream refuses to end
and you're courting euphoria or madness
whichever comes first.

Surreally Lucky in Love

You meet an attractive woman
bursting with intelligence
and hair that would have put
Medusa to shame
turns out she's from
another region or far-off locale
you're tempted to say another dimension
but why tamper with reality
and besides, you're being watched
so you turn your head
smile precisely
or what passes as a smile
return to thoughts
of loneliness
of damnation
of escape
to a place of seclusion
on the other side of time
or what passes as time
reality for you
if truth be told
has been tampered with
but you're no quitter
quite the opposite
and you have a trick or two
up your long sleeves
even as you leave
for another region or far-off locale
and you finally admit
to another dimension
where you dreamed of her
in the first place.

A Bus Commute Home

The late-afternoon commuter
fleeing an office that day after day
scrapes his soul, steals his time,
thinks a harsh mantra in rhythm
with the bus's grating movement:
the end of everything today
the end of everything tomorrow
the end of everything in a hundred years
the end of everything in a billion years ...

then mesmerized by the relentless second hand
of an old watch on the wrist of the young woman
standing next to him on the crammed bus
her left hand holding the overhead metal bar
his right hand tired from gripping too tightly
his thoughts find another destination

first the word *love* comforts him
then the word *eternal*
eternal love, he thinks
gripping even tighter
the bus almost dissolves
a film of his life revised:
courtship, marriage, a life together

the old watch disappears
as the young woman leaves
the bus a stop before his:
the end of everything today ...

Later That Night

He might ask if she'd ever lied during a prayer.
He might ask if she'd forgotten or forsaken love.
He might ask if she'd sought escape in deception.
He might ask if she'd sleep with a vagabond …

More likely, he'll pass her on the street
without a word or even a half-smile
but later that night, perhaps,
after he has run out of words and excuses,
they will have a lovely conversation
and one of them will fall in love.

A Cryptically Scented Envelope

If in youth
we are passed
a long letter
(within a cryptically
scented envelope
sealed half-lovingly
half-vindictively)
containing our last words
a drawing of our last love
a prayer for last hope
a photograph of a death mask
made by the most skilled hands
would we hide the envelope
in a safe place
and open it well
into old age
or rip the envelope
into forgetfulness
and write letters
of our own
passing them on
to the god of dreams
and resume
caressing the days?

The Beginning of Hostilities

Thank you for this
magnificent gift
perhaps I should say
munificent
the wrapping is
simply astonishing
but I am not worthy
or accustomed
to receiving gifts
from such celebrated
strangers
I've read about you
in the tabloids
seen your undamaged likeness
on television late at night
when I am afraid
of nearly everything
but why the rush
to open this gift
I can wait a year or two
please do not look at me
that mystifying way
it frightens me more
than the night
or the sound of gunfire
all around us.

Where to Hide?

Where were you
when all hell broke loose?
the sweetest voice
this side of Heaven
demanded to know
my file open
on a computer screen.

The night in question
I was on another planet
no need to be specific
specifics would shatter
the logistics of my hiding place
would leave me open
to sinister strictures.

Where will you be tomorrow morning?
asks the sweet voice growing gruff
as the serrations of Hell.

I was tired of thinking
of the wars and the warlike
tired of death tolls and sorrow
tired of the words for killing
and the killing of sense
so I fled like a cloud
sick of the rain
and found a corner of a planet
where killing and killers
are kept away.

Sit still, the questioning
is just beginning …

Until the Next Mid-Morning Voice Questions Me

Mid-morning, the minutes lenient,
yet the fence as I walked by
asked in dour earnestness,
"Do I hold in or keep out?"
Startled by the smooth diction
and refined accent
as much as the difficulty
of the mid-morning question
I was speechless
but made some hand gestures
to indicate both puzzlement
and a desire to communicate.
Again the fence spoke
this time in a gravelly voice
and an accent from a different world
asking without sympathy,
"Why do you walk near me?"
And words like tiny bullets
shot forth from me,
"You are not speaking
you are a liar of existence
a nonentity of inanimation
you are nothing but metal
and a design that reminds me
of my sadly spent youth."
As I began to walk away
the fence spoke rapidly,
"Then why are you afraid?
Why do you want to flee
to a safer confinement?"

I refused to stop
to turn or close my eyes
beginning a long prayer
that will accompany me
until the next mid-morning voice
questions me.

The Search for a Philosophy of Being Unrestrained

Before you demonstrate that you can fly
as well as any mythological figure
before you drive the earthbound nails
into the metaphorical coffin
before everything gets so messed up
—metaphors, chronology, memory—
and irrevocable as hell (or depictions of hell)
just take a few deep and symbolic breaths
whisper the name of any god you might find congenial
and enumerate a small portion of the reasons
flight is a blend of illusion and delusion.

Listen, I can do it for you, the enumerating,
the search for a philosophy for being unrestrained:
thinking, thought
seeing the unseen
something like music, like song,
something like love, loving
kindness and unkindness
a senseless thought after lovemaking
a few hours later almost made sense
like digging for artifacts, clues
to other civilizations
even if they harboured cruelty.

So, let us go get a coffee, my treat,
soaring through the clouds can wait
just as the end of the world or worlds
no need to become an artifact, a clue
to another's flightless philosophy.

Reassessment

If you live long enough
there is a point in every life
where you have forgotten more than you remember

in the measurement of memories
there is a point in every life
where you have the memory of more pain
than what you feel during those inexplicable moments
where you can believe in the miraculous

there is a point in every life
where your certainty about the days
is less than your uncertainty about nights

there is a point in every life
where you have the most words in your life
and the least ability to describe
what you have lost
or what was taken from you
by time and your own broken-heartedness

there is a point in every life
where the timeless is more appealing
than the accuracy of days and weeks

there is a point in every life
where the line between illusion
and absoluteness
is faded and untrustworthy.

One Person's Madness Is Another's ...

The cold winter's morning began
as uneventful as a home movie
filmed by a family of the invisible
(perhaps barely visible would be
more accurate, but it's early)
you dressed more for hopeful spring
than the season's sudden anger
as you walk past familiar houses
curtains drawn, addresses changed,
then quite by chance you discover
you don't exist, not in conventional terms,
hardly distressed, a little puzzled, though,
and immediately after you discover
two identical snowflakes
but you have no one to show these
inexplicable twins of nature
everyone huddled indoors
safe as the hearth personified
then with the naked eye
you discover a new planet
populated by creatures uncannily
similar to Godot, not that anyone
would believe you even if you claimed
the world was round and the sky blue
your credentials are lacklustre
your smile unimpressive
no one sees you, hears you even
when you use a megaphone
and yell passages from secret texts
you discover immediately after that
new planet and now you reassess

all your findings and descriptions
even as you find another planet
more distant and picturesque
populated by fantastical creatures
but you will not give these creatures
a name, not now, not anymore,
instead you will walk faster and farther
and find more identical snowflakes
for your collection of wonders.

You Can No Longer Spell *Immortality* with Your Eyes Closed

In your youth, close to its beginning,
you could spell *immortality*
with your eyes closed
but that's another thought
a little too unwieldy
for this line of thinking ...
Let me start again:
at the very emergence of a thought
not necessarily one momentous or multi-layered
merely a thought about the here and now
of consciousness and being
at the moment when a transformation begins
realization as a raindrop passing as a cloudburst
begins the start of a fleeing
or alternatively, the initiation of a descent.

First an ancient telephone
then a broken toaster
followed by several of your old thoughts
ones discarded when you learned
love was perishable
float through the room
this does not convince you
of magic or the miraculous
merely that time is cunning and
you can no longer spell *immortality*
with your eyes closed.

All This on a Night Anticipating Spectral Exclamations

Before I say there is no meaning or sense
before I yell there is no purpose or meaning
before I shout there is no sense or purpose
before I start to hurl words about wordlessness
before I start to cheat at existential card games
before I start to erase senseful images of nothingness
before I say yell shout hurl cheat erase
I will open my eyes, breathe with new abandon
and touch the smallest small notion of beauty
all this before I have a religious experience
all this before I endure an irreligious meltdown
all this before the cosmic knocks at my door
all this all this all this all this
on a night anticipating spectral exclamations
in languages I cannot comprehend
I offer, if I have anything to offer,
a sigh of relief if not of reverence
as magnificent as a single bird's song.

The Semblance of a Magical Life

It appeared in tiniest manifestation
innocuous and insignificant
as a flower in the shape
of a beggar's broken heart
unable to manoeuvre
wholeheartedly

this was neither absurd
nor divinely inspired
disobedience
it was a life unnoticed
until unfamiliar sounds became
louder as the sun rose
modestly

secretive words trickled forth
and laughed on their own
and somehow had sex
with other words
but metaphors were sorely lacking
that day as the ongoing light
crept into early darkness
but would not relinquish
the horror ahead

the tininess in disguise
grew and grew
like misshaped headlines
into mediocre madness
then something more massive
worse than a heart attack
or a rejection by eternity

then it begins all over again
you satisfied that madness
and its lovely attendants
add up to the semblance
of a magical life.

The Waiting Was for Naught

On a day raining meowing dogs and barking cats
Mister Run-of-the-Mill walks quickly
through the discordant business district
and is asked by a voice from above
certainly not an everyday voice
but hardly compelling or earth-shattering
a rather meek voice yet not unpleasant,
Do you want to speak to the Divine?

No, thank you, but I appreciate the thought,
Mister Run-of-the-Mill answers
and feeling strangely talkative, goes on:
I recall the last time I spoke to something
larger than myself and my meagre history
and we had nothing to say to each other
not a good joke, or a philosophical question,
or even a tidbit of titillating gossip
I recall standing there on an overcast day
not dissimilar to this one
of course I was much younger
full of piss and vinegar
but I waited and waited
to hear something
and then I waited and waited
to say something
and the waiting was for naught
and the silence enduring
until this very moment
and hearing your meek voice
yet again.

Other Skies in Other Places

It is an over-documented time
each second making as much sense
as each withering week and month
you look all around yourself
practising methods of detection
as a last resort looking upward
the sky or what used to be called sky
dripping confusion and memory
the confusion clever as night
the memory short of cleverness
and other skies in other places
you fearing night and its accomplices
going into a room away from sky
the walls painted as close
to blood-red as the word allows
the ceiling not a sky nor
a word for sky and night
and when you leave
a year or two later
having difficulty with time
as with skies and colours
seeking new colours
the world had changed
you deciding to call sky, *earth*
and earth, *sky*
and suddenly you could smile
before the sky falls on
you and your words
leaving you colourless.

For, Let Us Say, an Unflawed Half Day

If there were nothing
malicious
or sinful
or duplicitous
or iniquitous
no haughtiness
nothing surreptitious
no malevolence
or transgressions
even, for the sake of religion,
no pettiness
no tampering with souls
no chest-beating of the territorial
or domination by the rapacious
no belligerency whatsoever
for, let us say,
an unflawed half day,
we could love and dance
without the least restraint
not have to look over our shoulders
cover our asses
fortify our defences
distrust the knock at the door
then the half day would end
what was before would resume
and the flawed loving
and flawed dancing
would be sweeter
and truer than before.

All in a Day's Work

One morning, descending from sleep
and a not half-bad dream
about exploring and map-making,
you start to dig for a metaphor for Hell
dig assiduously, frantically
for reasons that have nothing to do
with digging or metaphors
calluses forming contrarily
you abandon digging
and attempt all afternoon
to perfect stumbling
toward an image of Heaven
nothing satisfying or substantial
morning or afternoon
nothing worth writing home about
or climbing to the top
of a mountain of clichés
so in the evening you visit the edge of eternity—
was it not pinpointed in a dream map
of yours, suddenly recalled?—
and start to sing madrigals
with a group of former celebrities
now dejected and forgotten
not that you've ever done that before
or even know what a madrigal might be
in your mind, you laugh at the futility
and the enormous foolishness
of your digging, stumbling, singing
and start to plan your next day
the morning, the afternoon, the evening

perfectly arranged, something like
an unblemished existential blueprint
until the digging, stumbling, singing
begin again and you long for sleep
and not half-bad dreams.

Thinking of Words

I went to bed
thinking the word *infinite*
and awoke with the word *finite*
rolling around my thoughts
like a sinister jester
performing not for mischief
but for wickedness.
Forget the previous image:
let me try again—
like a bemused deity
who wants to offer more
but always winds up
short changing
even the happiest
and the saddest
who think of words
during hopeful nights
and forsaken mornings.

As Mysterious as Elation

As I watched a bird
graceful as the word *flying*
said slowly and longingly
soar into the sky
the darkness dissolved
not into light or insight
but into a new mystery
as mysterious as elation.

I attempt to recall elation
the shapes of what is loved
the faces of those loved
I ask how many memories
are worth preserving
to deal with the darkness.

Then a suddenness of desire
for shapes and faces
the present burdened
under forgetfulness
the darkness re-emerges
and I think about thinking
the way a soaring bird
might think about flying
if the words were there
like the clouds
beckoning its ascent.

If We Didn't Have a Word for Beauty

Beauty is irrational.
No, beauty is as beauty does.
Unbeautiful
the opposite of beauty.
Is longing for beauty
the absence of beauty?
A life without beauty
a surfeit of beauty
a hundred words for beauty
beauty is wordless
beauty to the blind
imagining beauty
defining beauty
comprehending beauty
beauty as archetype
language, perception
if we didn't have
a word for beauty
or weren't forever caught
by the words of beauty.
Break the mirrors
erase the words
begin the portrait
over again.

Ugliness is irrational …

Meanings

I hear words from the weedful garden of a reclusive neighbour
misunderstood mumblings, I interpret, from cunning flowers
or even from scheming weeds aspiring to floral loftiness:
Are we dissolute because we're disillusioned
or are we disillusioned because we're dissolute?

As I consider the question and its voice
I hear laughter—
words I could accept from cunning flowers or scheming weeds
but the laughter seems to belong to something else
trees perhaps
trees I can imagine laughing
trees deep in forests away from
most things and sounds
with their cold-hard languages.

Is it time to question the voice
from the weedful garden
dispute its legitimacy
or is it time to get a new dictionary
and translate what is being said to me?

Misconstrued as the Sanity of Words

Underneath the words
just beneath the undergrowth
I found words of madness
misconstrued as the sanity of words.

How do you know this?
an exceedingly tall sceptic
just happening to be skipping by
asked me with a voice louder than thunder
if voices and thunder can be compared.

Just as I know oceans are huge
without an idea at measurement,
I answered, the start of a smile
on my previously smileless face.

Wrong! Not even close!
Inadequate response! Woeful answer!

Oh no, I think, not another denunciation,
a condemnation of my guessing at meaning
and the various shapes of existence.

Prayerful Advice

Put a hundred rarely used words
into a piteous magician's hat
kick out the rabbits and bad thoughts
brush away the lint and dandruff
and lost opportunities

have a snack first
maybe even a drink
strong or weak
expensive or homemade
won't help or hinder
what happens next

select ten words from the hat
read them aloud
in order of selection
and if you get a response
from God
count yourself lucky
or blessed
(apart from luck or blessings,
you notice in unmagical doubt
words that weren't in the hat
though on the tip of your tongue
now running circles around you
and your life of inaccuracy).

Put two hundred rarely used words
into a joyful magician's hat …

A New Word for Madness

I crouched and hid in a corner
of a room in a fortress that strangely
resembles a modest little house
on a street that could be
formed or malformed
in any of a hundred other eras.
It is self and its accomplices
searching for me
for reasons that stretch
as far as any horizon of madness.
Madness, that isn't the best description
much too overused in a world
that churns out madnesses
as if they were going out of style.
I want to make the world better
not as fragmented and unbalanced.
A new orbit, perhaps,
or different tides and length of days,
new, brighter nights
and less jarring days.
From my corner,
crouched like a scientist
who has forgotten all science
mistaken dreams for escape
I plan and plot
the saving of the world
and search most diligently
for a new word
for madness.

Undefined

I thought today
would have the same
rhythms and definitions
the customary shapes
and trickery that most
other days have as they
snarl and growl at me
days like intractable animals
but I am wrong for today
I turned into something
no one would have guessed
in a million days of guessing
and while the rhythms
and trickery of the change
are somewhat under control
I am still searching
for a new definition.

Time and Space

None of your watches or clocks
digital or analogue or magical
are working this morning
and you're scared because
this is your day to begin
to fly without wings
winged flight was too awkward
and besides, not natural
for a person to devise wings
and flap madly through
time and space
not that you can
keep track of the time
any longer but maybe
you will invent something new
for time-telling and keeping track
now that you can forget
about your cumbersome wings.

Escaping Absurdly

When you lose track of the days
but grip tightly to the seconds
and less than eager minutes

when you stumble while walking
but manage a short flight
a bit over the treetops

when you dissolve into something
more difficult to describe
than the past or lost love

you check your watch
change your shoes
and find a disguise
that fits all occasions.

The Logic of Absurdity

I wake to the chirping
of a large perturbed bird
devising a new dialect
a bird formerly fantastical
now as ordinary as my morning:
conundrum or dilemma
mystery or predicament
uncertain or unsure
not certain or not sure
quite obviously I'm
tied in metaphoric knots
tied up in metaphysical traffic
tied to an ancient mythology
uncertain as to the time of day
the lay of the land
the game's final score
who passed me on the street
the translation of the poem
the wild animal's ferocity
to look at Medusa or not
to be or not to be
this is getting absurd
correction, more absurd,
there was the deceit
of yesterday
and the day before
a disruption to my confusion
one hand clapping, yes,
I know that one
with certainty and surety

let me start again
this time with my hands
tied behind my back
a magician learning a new trick
afraid to go on stage.

Existential Inventory

Why do you bother
taking inventory
of your existence?
the woman asks him
when he shows her his list
of worldly items.

The man pauses
thinks a handful
of childhood memories
and crosses off one item
but adds two more
smiling for the first time
in a very unsatisfactory week.

Existential Calculations

What percentage of prayers
are answered
even partially?

What percentage of lottery tickets
are winners
even minimally?

What percentage of loves
are consummated
even imaginatively?

What percentage of fantasies
are realized
even half-formed?

What percentage of dreamers
are satisfied
even delusionally?

What percentage of acts of lunacy
are saving
even temporarily?

What percentage of questions
are answered
even deceptively?

Misstepping

A morning of ludicrousness
you get angry at anger
bitter at bitterness
decide to count all your regrets
become consumed by accuracy
that goes wrong beyond wrongness
you sign a letter of confession
that is so full of misspellings
any correctness becomes accidental
you characterize the morning
as one of miscounting
misspellings and so many missteps
believing you are on a vaudeville stage
somewhere in geography's
maligned past stepping here
stepping there misstepping
almost everywhere
the ludicrousness and inaccuracy
become so enormous
that getting back to the everyday
the blissfully ordinary
becomes more treacherous
than anger or bitterness
or even accuracy
you get angrier and angrier
more bitter than comprehensible
decide to take a long walk
and before the next morning
fall off the edge of the world
giving you half an eternity
by your own ludicrous estimate

to work on your counting
and spelling though
your feet no longer have
anything to step upon
misstepping finally
a thing of the past.

The Failed Philosopher's Quandary

Ignored or reviled?
the words flashing
on the neon sign
of your existence
you hardly eager
to choose this morning
too many metaphors
in the face of mortality
too many excuses
in the poorly lit room
of the interrogator
it is all so mysterious
once again, yet again
you are tired
tired of keeping track
of measuring and recording
details from the lives
of the nonexistent
it was a job, perhaps a task
a test by an authority
who loves failings
and harsh sentences
who adores mishaps
and unhappy endings.

Today, you think,
is the day for escape
but the stars are misaligned
the weather a little too balmy
you have profound thoughts to think
walls to contemplate
today it will be *ignored*
tomorrow, or the next day, *reviled.*

Memories of a Lucky Penny

Good-luck charms always brought him bad luck
or so he interpreted his attempt for a little assistance
during childhood and youth
from above or below or some little out-of-the-way locale

his tenth year, he recalls, was particularly luckless—
he fell off his bicycle with a rabbit's foot in his pocket
a summer in an cast

he lost his way gripping a four-leaf clover
and took three hours to get home
missed supper and was grounded
for three weeks, his mom's arithmetic

he was flipping his lucky penny
when he heard a voice from an old dented car invite him
for a treat and a ride
his penny fell to the sidewalk
rolling away as if it were a penny with a mind of its own
and he ran after that lucky penny losing its luck

later, at home, he heard his father,
caught by the evening news,
tell his mother about the terrible thing
that happened to a little boy two blocks away
an old dented car seen in the neighbourhood
and the luckless man visiting himself in memory
remembers telling them he saw that old dented car
but lost his lucky penny.

The Brokenhearted and Unrecognized Busker

The busker lived a life far away
from cities or acknowledgement
through dreams, bad and half-lovely
thoughts of being a singer of holy songs
thoughts of being loved
thoughts of being recognized
on a faraway street
the end was more than distance
more than failure
more than a falling away

offended by the night, frightened by the day
misunderstood by the hours, loathed by the seconds
it was a rather unwholesome adventure
through the alleyways and side streets
of a life or the semblance of a life

when the end came
as it did midpoint between
uproarious night and glaring day
the busker tried to sing something saving
instead a sad cacophony
that did catch God's ear
but undid or reshaped nothing
worth noting.

Contradictory

The waiter with the mystical smile
hands you a heavy menu
sharp-edged all around like barbed-wire regrets
and you cut your fingers in the opening
quickly make excuses for your bleeding
as if bleeding is unfashionable this time around.
I know what I want, you say,
holding the menu as a weapon
pointed at no one in particular:
I want truth, not a large portion,
my appetite is a bit out of sorts.
The waiter, a voice weary from repetition
and long double shifts, asks with a deadened smile:
How do you like your truths served up?
Full, succulent, flavourful,
or lean, painful, bitter?
On a silver tray shined for the occasion,
or thrown into the voiceless dirt?

I don't care, you say,
disliking verbiage
as you do overindulgence
in prayer or farewells.

The dead need truth also,
the waiter says
the smile coming alive
contradictory as a sudden affirmation of timelessness.
You start to disagree but pause in mid-thought
and wonder what truths you will need
when you leave this restaurant
having forgotten to eat.

A Song of the Gods of Madness

Even sitting at a restaurant table
his nervousness was as apparent
as a drummer trying to keep beat
to a song of the gods of madness.

There are no gods of madness
I can hear him say
as if he can read minds
and I wonder if the mad
are more intuitive than the firmly sane.

I am not mad
he says to everyone in the restaurant
and I take this as coincidence
an utterance of lifelong uncertainty
an inability to arrange or rearrange thoughts.

I order another coffee
and he calls from across the room
too much caffeine affects your nerves adversely
and with both hands holds up a glass of water
presenting his glass as if it were a chalice.

He stands, bows to the patrons and staff
as if he were a Shakespearean actor
fallen on hard times
but his timing is still impeccable
and he exits the restaurant
as if he knows exactly
what he is doing
and where he is going.

Tumbling in Memory

I take this tumble down the stairs
it's not like I haven't tripped before
but this time I fall below the bottom
to other worlds and times
must be some sort of endless falling
a sensation of bad dreams
and cunning guilt.

The pain does not begin
until a year later
as if an anniversary is required
for the pain and the memory of pain
tossing the words around
let them tumble
revisit your falling
in another bad dream.

I start to argue
it's not me who has fallen
only my memories
but the pain
puts a lie to that
and besides
I'm at the top of the stairs
a year later
and I take this tumble …

Time Running Out, Dreaming Truth

When a truth that keeps you from falling
into a land of lies and deception below
starts to clamour for bribes and flattery
you close your eyes and run full speed toward
whatever distance can accommodate you.

You would run faster if you could
but it is a night perfecting darkness
and your definition of light is inadequate
as inadequate as the best prayer you have to offer
in the night, time running out, dreaming truth.

Do you want to start over
forsake truth, find a better shaped lie
become a collector of falsehoods
and start making offers or threats
to former truths?

An Imagined Past and an Implausible Present

Sky-written in colours deep-kissing imagination:
AN OPPORTUNITY OF A LIFETIME
and in tiny print below
a phone number almost colourless.
Yes, I need an opportunity
my lifetime requires
an infusion of a heavenly offering.
A long walk home
thinking of the mundane
and of the miraculous
a dialogue with mystery
the mysterious growing
ordinary and indiscreet.
I reach my abode
where the opportunities
have faded and my lifetime
become something less.
I pick up my cellphone
shake it for luck
and tap in the numbers
as though my fingers are dancing
over the mundane and miraculous
and mysterious all at once
and then the ringing begins
a new-fangled prayer
I in my confusion
counting each and every ring
until the number becomes too high
to hold comfortably.
Seems like lifetime after lifetime passes
the ringing as rhythmic as breaths
or tiny little curses from unseen lips.

Finally, when all I have left
are an imagined past
and an implausible present
a voice more beautiful
than even the wind or thunder
tells me unequivocally
"The job has been taken by a magician"
and I register another lost opportunity
in my lifetime.

Counting and Recounting the Uncountable

Well, the world did not end
your dream was a false alarm
and a bad version of a B-movie
not even bad enough
to be cheesy or campy
or classifiable by adjective
or youthful memory
(the movies of your youth
like the songs and backseat necking
are another category altogether).

You close your eyes
after another day
of counting and recounting
the uncountable
and hope to hell
the world doesn't end
and tonight's movie
makes sense in the dark.

Spiritual Crisis

After prayer and praying
like drinking strong whiskey
a voice I feared to identify
surprised me with a question:

Would you rather be
unburdened or unearthly
when you leap into the chasm
of what comes next?

The question did not make
worldly sense but either did
the voice asking me
on a dismal mid morning
when faith and fancy
belief and disbelief
seemed to have a little
too much in common.

Ending Quandaries

Ready for the momentous
like a commercial
for immortality
and more?

Ready to be upstaged
like an actor
forgetting lines
and breathing?

Ready to die
like a nonentity
left out of everything
even God's mind?

Ready for more questions
like a sinner in hiding
perfecting sin
and repentance?

The Old Photograph

No one in the living room could recall
when the old photograph
appeared on the wall near the door
was there an older photograph
anywhere in the family
in the city even
but now, a family reunion's
last few moments
someone, drink in hand,
comments that he was a bastard
and lived to be a hundred
another, grabbing coat
and at the door
says he died at eighty in his sleep
and was that age in the photo
another says ninety-five, if a day,
guesses left and right
from early sixties to late nineties
in bed, drowned, murdered, off a cliff,
hanged, poisoned, accident, conspiracy,
self-inflicted gunshot wound,
a little boy saying two hundred
and I want to go home.
He was a good generous man
who lived an upstanding life
in tough and unforgiving times
a seafaring man on the open seas
a recluse in an old shack
a bastard, a lousy bastard,
the "lousy" added with another drink.

His great-granddaughter
a woman now approaching ninety
was helped to the wall with the photo
and looked up at the mysterious face:
I met him once and still remember
where he touched me.

She Is About to Push Him into Silence

Your timing was untimely, she said,
sneering at her own words.
A timeless threat, he thought,
fearful of her look
more than her words delivered
like an actress angry at acting.

If this were a play
and they were on stage
he could smile and
they could go have a drink
afterward, discuss all
that went wrong
—missed cues
mangled stage directions
flubbed or forgotten lines
inaccurate or false emotions—
smooth things out
a naturalistic play
or even an absurd one
he wasn't all that fussy
with his images of restoration
he knew she never had much time
for comedies and anything
with a contrived happy ending.

But this is the edge of something
irrevocable, frightening
and she is about
to push him into silence
and impose her dream
of flight and no one
is in the audience
to save either of them

An Outlandish Life Out of Context

The interrogator
larger than life
weapons at hand —
was it in a dream
or an alleyway?
in broad daylight
or the dead of night? —
a justification of being
demanded on the spot:

out of context
out of touch
out of hearing
out of sight
out of sorts
out of it
out of place
out of fashion
out of here
out of time
out of words
out of body …

He was found
out and out dead
the next day
in an alleyway
by a mute
who a minute before
was wondering
what she would say
if asked about
her unbroken silence.

Of Fate and Regret and a Forthcoming Obit

A day unlike any other
thinks the unphilosophical, jovial man
who usually doesn't think such thoughts
radiant, glorious, a record-high temperature
for a mid-winter early afternoon
just the slightest breeze
to remind one of weather
and worldly movement
then he breathes deeply
deeper than he has ever breathed
and feels lightheaded
lighter headed than he has ever felt
inspired, uplifted, he begins to run
run faster than he has ever run
faster than the impatient cars
along the busy street he has chosen
for his sense-defying run
as he runs, faster and faster,
he recites poems he doesn't recall
reading or hearing
sings songs from his youth
vaguely recalled
yet the words exact
recites and sings clearly, loudly
louder than the impatient cars
honking at him
at his breathtaking speed
at his precise recitations
at his loud singing.

Sad to say, the day unlike any other
for the unphilosophical, jovial man
in a few seconds would become his last
but no need to tell him of fate
and regret and a forthcoming obit
let him run and recite and sing.

Existential Futility

Bad enough yesterday, after only two glasses of whiskey,
and cheap whiskey at that,
you got the days mixed up, Wednesday for Friday,
the theological with the downright earthy,
and then another day, something stronger,
you got two decades mixed up
even two clearly defined decades
and from that sort of chronology
you went on to even earlier events
historic and not so historic
mixing up the sad and the happy
the soul-puncturing and the spirit-uplifting
and as the evening progressed
a few friends sitting there in your
damaged room, complaining and crying
as if you were listening and had the proper medicine
and on another day, a day with horrible weather
that made the television forecasters bite their tongues
until they drew blood and lost articulateness
then throw themselves off studio cliffs
you mixed up war after war after war
and tried in the end to recite a poem
that set everything in order
the chronology and the events
and even the wars
but you failed as miserably
as someone holy trying first to speak with God
and then, even more futilely,
to speak with the opposite of God.

A Hungry Creature That Hates Fast Food

You meet a hungry creature
that hates fast food
expressing a desire
for synapses and psyches
in a holistic sandwich
or mixed into a healthy salad
with a zesty spirit dressing.

You're somewhat peckish yourself
you tell the creature
who says hungry
is too mild a word
for its ravenous state.

Ravenous isn't a word
you find appetizing
you tell the ravenous creature
as it moves closer to you
licking what looks like lips
but you can't be sure
frightened as you are
having lost your appetite.

A Frightening Metaphysical Puzzle

When confronted by the stranger
demanding answers or else
a fate worse than death
is it better to be philosophical or practical
honest or deceptive?

The stranger, I should add,
is unearthly and sinister
with a gunlike apparatus
you don't recognize
but assume is as functional
as any worldly weapon.

The questions, of course,
strain your intellectual grasp
and lifetime of this-planet experience,
questions that even astute theologians
and proficient game-show contestants
would have difficulty with.

Trembling, you answer question
after question, adrenaline somehow
conjuring up knowledge and wisdom
stumble on the tenth one
a frightening metaphysical puzzle
and pray that the gunlike apparatus
isn't loaded.

Coffee Stains

As I write this poem
I have a newly formulated
theory that somewhere
in the world
there is another person
writing a poem
very similar
to this one
maybe with a little less
angst
and a little more
serenity
but otherwise
very close
same number of lines
a parallel image
or metaphor
even a coffee stain
on the page
but I cannot confirm
this theory
I can only keep
writing
until I run out
of coffee or steam
and then make myself
another coffee
and devise
another theory.

An Absurdly Disrupted Poet Hides Behind a Bookcase

No, oh no, heavens no, please no,
here they come to my front door
the authorities and the experts
one after another in profusion
the rhythm of their arrivals
incontrovertible—
yes, at least ten of them
drove to here in convertibles
big noisy engines, flashy colours
but none appreciates
the coincidence of the incidents
that's not quite right,
not precisely or accurately—
what the strategic hell
I have to deal with them here and now
the authorities and the experts
one after another arriving
I feel disrupted, absurdly disrupted,
and I want to be scribbling poems
and prayers and drawing maps
for the way out of this house
before more authorities and experts
come to my front door—
I'll hide behind a bookcase
like a criminal in the night
(a metaphor-criminal in the metaphoric night)
and wait until the authorities and the experts
tire of knocking at my front door
then I'll return to the world
an animal breaking free
of its snare and cruel sentence.

A Precise Calculus of Near Poetic Death

At a newly renovated bar
windowless as perfected darkness
midtown fading midafternoon
the former poet (definition his)
like a huge honourable mention
from a befuddled judge
claims he has no more
than five beers a day
(but no less, mind you)
a precise calculus
of near poetic death
then utters, a bit of foam
at the corner of his mouth,
"Mourning for the lost morning,"
and laughs, says today he will
shatter the calculus
if I buy him a sixth beer
I say yes, compassion or pity
(difficult to diagnose)
bring up the play title
Mourning Becomes Electra
he guesses Eugene O'Neill
(surprise-quiz impressive)
and I leave before
the former poet finishes his beer
or comes up with another line
of broken poetry.

Artificial (Poetry) Intelligence, *or,* A Luddite's Lament

How does it happen
that it happens
when it happens?

Do me and posterity
a favour of poetic grandeur
and shut the hell down.

How does it happen
that it happens
when it happens?

Enough already
you spurious machine
of uninspired utterances.

How does it happen
that it happens
when it happens?

Cease and desist, cease and desist,
for God's sake, cease and desist,
or I'll smash you to smithereens.

How does it happen
that it happens
when it happens?

I have fists of words
the words of fists
and I will obliterate you.

How does it happen
that it happens
when it happens?

Yes, but my blood is now on you
a heartfelt message to eternity
on a deranged canvas of absurdity.

. *How ... does ... it ...*

Forgotten Sleep

In a crevice of the night
the pompous battle the pious
a nonsensical game
a replica of sanity
but what can you do
when you quarrel with
larger-than-life gods

perhaps if you curse
into the darkness
the darker the better
painting both reality
and illusion
with similar colours

now sit at your desk
in the dark fashioned
from long-past nights
and begin to list
reasons for sleeping
at inopportune times
for preferring a clever word
for darkness
to the inescapable.

Imaginary Distances

The distance between
worth and worthless
when you're measuring
memories and regrets
isn't all that distant

the distance between
sense and senseless
when you're measuring
absurdity and madness
isn't all that distant

the distance between
life and lifeless
when you're measuring
redemption and salvation
isn't all that distant

there, a life lived
measured accurately
or inaccurately
it hardly matters
at beginning or end.

Ordinariness

You have maps of Paradise
however imprecise
quite the collection.

You have recordings of God
however distorted
never reaching radio airplay.

You have memories of perfection
however imperfect
an exile from sanity.

You have dreams of madness
however fearful
a return to belonging.

You have obits of the invisible
however succinct
a catalogue of eternity.

You have albums of photos
however authentic
proof of nothingness.

Unforeseen Laughter

Their cellphones ring
simultaneously
a sinister operatic duet
her husband, of course,
his wife, probably,
neither lover answers
the ringing ceases
simultaneously.
A moment before
their lovemaking
coded, exhilarating,
beautifully crafted
false names
lovely shaped pasts
and accomplishments
something approaching
happiness at the most
regeneration at the least.
Then the scars
unnoticed earlier
perhaps it was the unanswered
ringing, perhaps the curtains
being opened and the unexpected
street activity, a hundred strangers.
Her quiet day
turned disquieting
his satisfying existence
turned dissatisfying
all in the time it took
to forget the exact
contour of madness.

Next week, same time,
he says, a slight smile.
I won't bring my cellphone,
she says, unforeseen laughter.

Personal Mythology

She asked me on the day
her madness officially ended
why such darkness
in the middle of the day
shows all her betrayals
and such brightness
in the middle of the night
taunts her senses and memory.

I have no answer
no sweet reprieve from anything
but she will not move
leave my path
and she is as strong
as ten ferocious men
and as adamant
as a deity refusing
to leave its holiest shrine.

I need to find all I have lost
the small, sad items
and the large, difficult
to identify ones,
I say, part entreaty
and part admission
of humiliation.

She disappears as adroitly
as she had appeared
and already I miss
her strength and adamancy
walking forward to a different time's
geography and chronology
hoping for another stranger
worthy of devotion.

A Far-Travelling Handwritten Love Letter

A man alone in a bomb shelter for five,
formerly handsome, nearly forty looking fifty
from loneliness and fear and disassembled dreams
starts a letter with a line learned as a child
heartfelt loving words from a mother's lullaby
working his way through a long love letter
full of words in careful yet cramped order
a plea, more or less, for love,
salvation, forgiveness, reprieve,
he's lost in the words learned during a lifetime
of lost lullabies replaced by harsh songs
of pursuing love and salvation
and forgiveness and reprieve.
The man inserts the long letter
into a wine bottle he had been saving
for better days, even bearable days,
a bottle for two to celebrate love
or the end of hostilities
they will end, have to end,
he whispers to the walls
the wine finished like the letter
in haste but with strange hopefulness
he leaves his fortified hiding place
walks the deserted streets to the water's edge
and hurls the bottle toward another world.

A woman, a hundred years hence,
walking along an isolated beach
off limits, still contaminated, yet she dares
sick of restrictions and hiding
amazed not by the distance or sentiments
the itemized desires, glorification of love

or heartfelt loving words
from a mother's long-ago lullaby
but by the numerous misspellings
and neatly printed address of a city
that no longer exists.

No One Believed She Was That Old

She wrote 500 erotic poems
in 500 years
of toil and hiding
relentless in imagining
the cruel magic
of the sensual
she admitted there were
unscrupulous exchanges
with malformed versions
of the demonic
how else could she describe
the perfection of madness
no one believed
she was that old
not 500 years
or appreciated what she wrote
except one lonely-shaped man
who craved affection
as much as immortality
and was willing to write
anything for anyone
even a malformed
collector of souls
standing nearby
where one enters sleep.

Time to Leave

What's all this crap about monotony and tedium?
asks a voice hidden within the revelry
the music loud as memory
memory louder than bad dreams.

Just trying to evaluate my existence
in this low-ceilinged bar.

Look at the wall pictures of the newsmakers
high achievers, smooth skinned,
at least from here, our corner booth.

Undeniable that I'm closer to death
than to fantasies and unimaginable escapes.

Maybe you should try praying
I could suggest some words
remember, at school,
I could hurl those jewelled words
skyward and inward
broke my share of hearts
last thing you broke was that beer glass
two nights ago.

I was frightened
when I saw an old friend
she died last year in my arms
breathing tricked and prayerless.

Time to leave, gentlemen,
the bartender says
but in a voice
lost to chronology.

When Will They Break Down Your Door?

You confront night's onset, yet another night,
with yet another question stabbed by mortality
or is it merely Kafkaesque trembling
and shadowy historical wandering:
When will they break down your door?

You sense it will be a darker than average
night with strong sounds abounding.
You've been wrong before especially
with God looking over your shoulder
but sometimes you have to go
with your hunches and broken prayers.

Will they wait until you have stumbled
upon the secrets of silence and love?

Will they wait until you have come apart
and lost the instructions for re-assembly?

Will they wait until they need a memory
or a lie to deal with *their* demons?

Will they accept your bribe of adulation
or even a semblance of a confession?

Will they steal your adroitness
from you and your saving memory?

Will they demand you rename
love and madness and memory?

Will they demand you turn your back
on shadowy history and Kafka's worlds?

Will they knock down the wrong door
and you will have another night?

Will your luck finally change
just when the end is about to be?

At the Midpoint Between Heaven and Hell in a Dismal Barroom

Heavenly has nothing to do with Heaven
because there is no damn Heaven,
you whisper before your first drink
philosophy and theology and predictions
of vile discoveries and vulgar endings
will come later, second or third drink,
the night is young, your intellect
hardly lubricated, apocalyptic chatter awaits.
On some nights revelations and wisdom
flow early before your drinking partner
talks of self-destruction or rebirth
or a deep understanding of nothing
and its multiplicity of corollaries
even of compassion and love and regret
like cheap food additives gone poisonous
the conversational mix more than madness
the darkness cultivated, refined, redefined,
and magically misshaped, further darkened.
I know I'm not qualified to deal with your mind
but what the heck, have another drink on me
you've earned it, what with your stirring avoidance
and marvellous sidestepping all so eloquently displayed.
As I leave, eager for silence and escape,
I hear you order another drink
and yell into the dismal barroom,
Hellish has nothing to do with Hell
because there is no damn Hell ...

Old Sci-Fi Films

All the elderly man
nearing a hundred now
watched were old sci-fi films
from the 1950s and 60s
a collection of videos
the envy of any film buff
over and over, nothing else
not sitcoms or the evening news
his favourite *Plan 9 from Outer Space*
for reasons beyond irony or sense
claiming Bela Lugosi
was a cherished friend.

The film-watching elderly man
ate well and frequently
though mainly whole-grain bread
drank skim milk by the jug
kept up his spirits
by singing in a language
no one in the seniors' home
recognized
waiting for them to land
on the lawn of the seniors' home
and take him back
to a planet
where age was irrelevant.

During each viewing
he laughs several times
describes the beauty
of his childhood home

its complexity and richness
and pointing at the common room's
larger-than-life TV screen
tells everyone in the room
they got it all wrong
not even close,
those silly, silly Earthlings.

On This Outlying Planet

Here I am on this outlying planet
no name yet
but nameless things
especially planets
always irritate
and naming must be done
like breathing or complaining
about eternal things.

The trip wasn't so bad
not like in sci-fi films.
Should I remove my spacesuit
breathe the air of this outlying planet?
It could be purer or worse
than my previous planet
but why take a chance
my spacesuit is state of the art
and I have a lifetime supply
of the best manufactured air
money can buy.

Maybe I won't leave my spacecraft
maybe I will sit here
with my protective spacesuit
and look through the portal
at this outlying planet
no longer outlying
because I am finally here.

Maybe I will name it *Earth*
or *Imagination*
or leave it nameless
I am not sure yet
being new to space travel
and landing on outlying planets.

The *We Never Close* Neon Sign

I won't necessarily be there
when the world expires
with a difficult to describe
cacophonous amalgam
of whimpering-banging
(or T. S. Eliot's simple whimper)
but my doppelgänger
surely will be in attendance
you know, at the tavern
with the *We Never Close* neon sign
that I find brazenly poetic
have photographed in both
vivid foreboding colour
and in revealing black-and-white
the windows boarded in
from being broken too many philosophical times
(or should I say existential or absurd times
that's also poetic if not prophetic)
the beer warm more often than cold
but the prices best in town
the bartenders and servers
more infernal than eternal
the tavern talk drowning in nostalgia
makeshift personal flotation devises
shaped out of sadness and regret
everyone singing of bygone times
yet no one wears a watch
expensive or otherwise
no one embraces calendars
accurate or speculative
but when it happens
it will be déjà vu for all the patrons

however ever after, the world will end
neither with whimpering déjà vu
nor with banging déjà vu.
but a cacophonous amalgam
(I repeat myself)
that's my theory, at least,
but you'd have to ask my doppelgänger
his theory, because he will be there
at the tavern with the *We Never Close* neon sign
drinking warm beer and a smile of escape
that he'll not have to pay his tab
onerous as eternity.

On the Set of a Minor Motion Picture

I've seen too many movies in my uneventful life,
the movie-star handsome man
at the bar said to the bartender,
his words three-whiskies loud
his smile threatening to consume his face
like special-effects in a not-so-subtle
horror movie.

A woman three bar stools away
having already had three husbands
who weren't half as handsome
as the befuddled barroom actor
said she prefers plays to films
unless they're foreign films
for which she has
an almost erotic weakness
pronouncing the word *erotic*
the way Marlene Dietrich might have
in *The Blue Angel.*

What the hell's the difference between a movie and a film?
asks an argumentative man sitting at the end of the bar
who looks like four or five of Lon Chaney's
thousand movie or film faces mixed together
and sounds like a character played by Boris Karloff.

Then a couple enter
sunglasses and prettiness
and studied self-importance
and the bartender
and the movie-star handsome man
and the thrice-divorced woman

and the argumentative drinker
all at the same moment realize
that real honest-to-goodness movie stars
have entered the bar and their lives
but they all guess different names
even though one of the entering actors
had been in four scandals in the last two years
and if any of them had just kept their eyes open
in the tabloid-emblazoned grocery check-out line
he or she would have guessed correctly.

But If You Lived Your Life Differently

The two on the street corner
were having a shouting match
perhaps a love affair on its last leg
or the prelude to darker embraces
one started to sing a martial song
stirring the blood, stroking memory,
the other began to dance
a poor version of a 1920s flapper
(defiant, sexual, devouring)
in one of those movies
you know is not real
but if you lived your life differently
you'd go to a secretive little bar
a welcoming speakeasy, let's say,
have three or four drinks
with a time-defying flapper
and tell the woman how much you adore
the brooding, complex films of Ingmar Bergman
and she tells you her older sister
sleeps with swaggering gangsters
and is about to be in a motion picture
sure to be all the rage.

Suddenly, like the slap from a jealous lover,
you realize you're a lonely anachronism
without any makeup or a good line
that would break the heart
of a time-defying flapper
or her older sister.

A Murmur of Sorts

In the midst of history
I hear an announcement
as loud as destiny:
The cameras and microphones are here.

In the midst of a fading morning
I hear a voice
as loud as a mythic creature's:
I believe in my heart of hearts
we are remembered
by the warnings we heed
the dissolutions we sidestep
the hells we redefine and rearrange
and the confessions we utter.

History and the morning
frighten me into silence
into a bafflement of being.

What, you are not a celebrity
or a historical figure
no never mind
confessing is of the essence
like breathing or hiding
in times of chaos
confess, confess, confess
consequences are dire.

I break my silence with a murmur of sorts:
But I hardly exist …

There, don't you feel better?

Despite Being Weaponless

I love a good joke
within a bad dream
as much as anyone
facing a stranger
holding a gun
and eager to make
the evening news
just once.

That's humour,
wouldn't you say,
but I'm not the one
on stage, so to speak,
in the limelight,
so, since you seem to be
at odds with authenticity
and between psychoses,
tell me a good joke
within my bad dream
not too funny
nor convoluted
something earthy
a real knee-slapper
as a famed theologian
I knew in my youth
used to say but he never
knew how to laugh
not at new-world jokes
and he always missed
his target thinking
of the old world.

I, on the other hand,
am a good shot in dreams
despite being weaponless
but bored to surreal tears
so let's hear the joke
before I have to deal
with my anonymity
and damaged sense
of wakeful humour.

A Scavenger of Words

Idiomatic idiotic remarks
as the clock tick-tocks away
into the memory of time.

What does that drivel mean?

Perhaps I should have said,
or even sang out,
Idiotic idiomatic remarks,
the order, you know,
is meaningful
and full of meaning.

You should be fed to carrion eaters
that have no time for words
only for feeding on fools.

Birds of prey or praying birds
would that be?

You and your language,
nothing but a scavenger of words.

Are you the idiom or the idiot?

I am silence and time
and I have captured you.

Not as long as I collect words
and arrange them one by one
on that timeless saving something
resembling a lover's heart
and a path away from captivity.

For Reasons Surreal and Absurd

On the third Thursday
of the second cruellest month
your morning ruminations
of surreal love without any thought
of absurd love
of absurd truth without any thought
of surreal truth
devour the surreal and the absurd
when everything is going well
in your strange-getting-stranger life
but not in the strange-getting-stranger life
of your doppelgänger
who parts his hair differently than you
and rarely replaces the toothpaste cap
otherwise you two
are almost indistinguishable
like two characters
from a short but frightening play
by a playwright
who changed his name
to Alfred Jarry
for reasons surreal and absurd
and believes in love and truth
unequivocally
on the third Thursday
of every second month.

Poetry-Reading Honorarium

When a space alien feels alienated,
the outsider poet
(or is it the underground poet?)
yells at the start
of a well publicized reading
pauses like a poetic deer
caught in the headlights
of a luxury car
the audience waits
for the next line
the foray into absurdity
but silence
and a few vague coughs
fill the little library
on the outskirts
of Heaven.

The outsider and/or underground
poet imagines a reading
in Hell and smiles
comfortable in the thought
and starts to count those
in the audience
for the report he has to submit
to a granting agency
that comprehends
neither Heaven nor Hell
but will send him an honorarium
to an address he is about
to make up.

Intergalactic Alphabet Sounds

Sci-fi films and stories aside,
you wonder where they will first land
centre of a big bustling city
or a corner of a sad small town
where nothing spectacular happens
knowing there are suburbs and deserts
villages and lakeside resorts
skyscraper-vexing cities galore
hills and valleys here and there
congested and sparse habitats
the possibilities abound
but what if they decide to land
in your driveway with no forewarning
luck or unluck of the draw
then it happens, dream or reality
who's keeping track …
you recently awoke
after a rough day
of everything going wrong
you and the other standing there
two disoriented beings
looking at each other up and down
suspicion flowing everywhere
you're too shy to speak first
and the other too tired from space travelling
you both say nothing for the longest time
time and history merrily going on
the hustle and bustle, to-ing and fro-ing,
the other being
speaks first in a voice quite soft
and the language, while perplexing,
has some interesting alphabet sounds

or what you assume are letters of an alphabet
intergalactic as they might be
and you seem to hear the words
"This is disappointing"
and you whisper "Your place or mine,"
waiting for redemptive laughter
or something that says
the world is not about to end.

A Lifetime of Headlines and Confusion

Curiosity about the curious creature
appearing and disappearing
atop the hat of the sorrowful person
walking back and forth
like a soldier from an ancient war
on the street of fashionable boutiques
and well-crafted gallows.

"It does make sense,"
the voice through the megaphone proclaims
the confusion and dread concealed
but what the magic metaphoric hell
our discernment is drenched in alcohol
and a lifetime of headlines and confusion.

During a lull from the hellishness of special effects
one of the shoppers, name brands like nooses, yells,
"Turn up the radio news louder
let's hear who is invading where
geography and dissolution are newsworthy."

One last chance to flee this fortification
our identity papers will be checked
and our forgeries wouldn't fool a foolhardy fool
we will be asked about the curious creature
and the type of hat it dances upon
we will answer with a prophecy of a future calamity
and a short but accurate description of a past sadness
as if we invented history and do not fear its disarray.

The Forlorn Creature's Lament

The forlorn creature
of impressive size
and lofty countenance
stands at the street corner
aged but with the streaming hair
of an immortal youth
bellowing out in a voice
louder than ten frightened humans,
I have no one to talk to
not a soul to speak with
no deities of wisdom
no friends of loving mirth
no confidants of sinister levity
no strangers with broken weapons
an aloneness of legendary shape
just a lifetime of memories
of those humans who hunted me
I miss your pursuit
I miss your weapons
I miss your cruelty.

Voices in an Especially Ominous Night

When you hear voices
(voices almost like visions
almost like frightened animals
given voice, fleeing wilderness)
in an especially ominous night
you trapped by fitful sleep,
by deceived sleep, by sleeplessness,
voices as yells, screams, shouts,
the roaring of confusion,
as whispers articulate and inarticulate,
in other languages, words from other worlds,
other times, other regrets, otherness as diction,
as warning, as wistfulness, as love even,
voices enhanced, augmented,
voices in a film about someone else's life
and exploits and misshapen fate
voices authentic and inauthentic
the differences between them
in this especially ominous night
hardly worth enumerating
voices disguised, reviled
voices alterable, revocable
voices before humiliation
before mortification
before the degradation
of dispirited mortality
before the beginning of time
rehearsed for the end of time
you lie there and listen
your mind some sort of
recording device

ready to play it all back
when the time comes for wordlessness
and proving the voices wrong …
you did belong
just like the especially ominous night
and all the godly and ungodly voices.

In a Different Time and Place, It Could Have Been Love, but Instead …

How late in life they met
romantic broken like branches
in an indifferent storm
too many harsh winters
and less than satisfying summers
both with drinks in hand
"I have a mountain of regrets,"
she said, looking upward,
"I have an ocean of regrets,"
he said, looking downward
she had a gun, he a knife,
a bad film noir, certainly,
but in a different time and place
it could have been love
but instead they exchanged weapons
laughed about regrets
drank even more
words tumbled out of their thoughts
there was lovemaking
there was senseless talk of a future
the past kept intruding
like those harsh winters
and less than satisfying summers
one almost smiled
the other cried
each became the other's past.

Excavation

You dig and dig
at first casually
soon inexorably
in your formerly tidy
backyard
finding not bones
or treasure
but rumours
and threats
not of eternity
or even reprieve
but of stillness
and emptiness
and a hint of
where to dig next
until digging is divine
and you are at the centre
of worship.

Furtive Yet Fascinating

There are days when one should not speak
at least not to those in physical form
days when words should be shared
with only the formless and featureless
those whose identities slide off them
like the rain off the smoothness
of million-year-old rocks
near or at the top of imaginary mountains.

Speak up, speak up, the silence declares
on one of those furtive days,
furtive yet fascinating, you think,
and you believe you have nothing to say
to save your life or the lives
of those worshipping imaginary mountains—
the silence not deafening, merely mystifying,
yet the silent conversations begin
words overtaking your thoughts and disquiet
despite you, in spite of you,
and end without the world ending
or your lips moving.

When Words Are Most Needed

In the dead of night
in the dead of winter
when words are most needed
like love or whiskey
for sense and warmth
and light's embrace,
a startling coincidence—
and isn't your absurd life
most overtaken by coincidence
in winter and in night—
yes, a startling coincidence
strikes you and the universe
almost at the same instant
when God devises the perfect metaphor
for the excuse of your stumbling being
and you come up with a near perfect
metaphor for God's existence
not that stumbling you or God
are especially magical poets
though you have lied yourself
into poetic ecstasy and worthiness
searching for a new nurturing word
for the dead of winter
and a new stronger word
for the dead of night
to complete the last line
of your latest winter verse
or perhaps a future nighttime poem.

Existential Texting

Everyone should text messages
to their former selves
all the consciousnesses
altered, lost, or stolen

everyone should text messages
to their future selves
all the consciousnesses
imagined, found, or returned

in despair or elation
all the former and future selves
disavowing texting
and all electronic devices
should reply in a formal hand
with letters explaining
what went wrong
or will go wrong
so the entrance to wherever
consciousnesses go
can make a tiny bit of sense
or, at the very least,
leave a record of being.

The Art of Becoming Invisible

Why doesn't anyone answer
my well composed inquiries
sent at every solstice, equinox,
and partial or full eclipse,
punctually year after year?

Why doesn't anyone answer
my succinct yet solemn prayers
when cacophony is approaching myth
periodically here and there?

Why doesn't anyone see
my impressive touching of the moon
during less than desirable nights
haphazardly once in a while?

And why does that figure with the gun
yell at me to turn around
just as I've mastered
the art of becoming invisible?

The Literary Scholar's Retirement

Not far from his former office
which overlooks not only
what he had accumulated and discarded
but greenery of immense imagination
the literary scholar is talking to a large animal
blessed with speech and hunting prowess
that has written a treatise on retribution.

The literary scholar wants to exchange ideas openly
yet secretly wanting secrets revealed
an explanation for the mythic and magical
but fearful as superstition to ask
the largeness of the animal
intimidating if not mystifying.

Then the large animal asks the literary scholar
about his opinions of the deadly confrontation
of intruding humans and wild animals in films
about wilderness and exploration
adapted from nineteenth-century novels.
The nineteenth century is my century,
the literary scholar says by way of apology
desiring time travel in either direction.

The Frightened Magician's Final Performance

There at the front of the stage
a frightened magician begins to perform
one more anxious trick
the night has been long and disappointing
the tricks and trickery
getting more convoluted
than an inveterate swindler
reminiscing over a lifetime
of seeking the beauty of deception.

I will make a ghost appear
and offer solace and consolation
I will make a ghost take earthly form
and offer a million sweet proofs,
the frightened magician says,
sweat on his straining brow
knowing the weight of last chances—
in the midst of the most sonorous
abracadabra words I'd ever heard
he drops dead and hits the floor
like a discarded prop
or a perfect clattering curse.

Everyone in the audience
goes home with a new memory
and something to talk about
for at least a day or two.

On a Day All the Prayers Sounded Too Sad and Insubstantial

On such a day
I walked out the door
half naked and fully amused
by the stillness and madness
that were tugging
at each other's sleeves

On such a day
I mistook nearly everything
except a lie I once told myself
about beauty and the world
going on forever

On such a day
I rearranged the words
of an old prayer
so it sounded like a lullaby
that once dispelled
all my childhood fears

On such a day
I caught the sky
as it fell unpredictably

On such a day
I contemplated praying

On such a day ...

Learning the History of War

As a child, keen on learning history
even from its frightening pages,
during a classroom discussion
of warfare and its endless sadness
you spoke out of turn, class disrupter,
and the teacher ordered you
to write the names of every war
on the chalkboard, watch spelling.

You spent half your youth writing the names
and escaped the classroom before
you were a fraction of the way through
whereas God, who much more often spoke out of turn,
was ordered to write the names of all the war dead
combatants and innocents
and is still at the chalkboard
writing in sorrow and mourning.

On the Outskirts of Mars Where No One Ever Dies

You dreamed
of an old woman
who dreams of writing
a long love poem
on the outskirts of Mars
where no one ever dies
a woman who never married
or left her hidden town
a woman who almost
ran away, early 1940s,
with a handsome soldier
a soldier whose body
was unrecognizable
you know the tragic story
and war's cruelty
her war never ended
love poem never completed
least not in her hidden town
sadness overwhelming
remembering by coercion.

Now she dreams
of writing a long love poem
on the outskirts of Mars
and forgetting that part
of her long life
without love.

A Distant Planet Full of Walls and Words for Walls

The Earthling travelled
to a distant planet full of walls
a rather long interplanetary
journey but it was a slow life
and worth going that distance
through time and space.
After the initial acclimatization
the walls started to preoccupy
the recently arrived Earthling
who began to tap at a nearby wall
then a little harder soon much harder
and amazingly, miraculously
the first wall started to crumble
and he thought of Joshua
and the Battle of Jericho
walls tumbling in the memory
of a childhood Biblical story
and in his mind he heard a gospel singer
singing "Joshua Fit the Battle of Jericho"
and he sang along in the silence of space
but that was ancient history
and he was caught in a walled present
tapping at walls one after another.
Wall after wall on this distant planet
crumbled, fell, became debris
both literarily and symbolically
for the Earthling still thought
in Earth terms and the memory of words.
The Earthling counted the walls
he had undone
for no other reason

than he felt walled in, confined
a hundred times worse
than on Earth:
five, ten, fifty walls
the first day,
fifty more the second day
and every day after that
for the first month
the first year
the first decade
and after a while all the Earthling
could think of was returning home
his thoughts discursive and almost
beyond sense
searching for the tallest wall
dreaming about the smallest wall
the words of walls, walled language
the words for wall,
the Earthling thought,
were walls in themselves
so on and on and on
a world of walled thoughts
and the Earthling prayed
to the gods of walls
to return him to his beloved Earth
but no one responded
and the Earthling resumed
tapping at the distant planet's walls
wondering if he had travelled
to Heaven or to Hell
the walls of thinking
even in the silence of space
more numerous than ever.

The Tactical Unit's Sharpshooter Misses His First Shot but Not His Second

Darkness obscures everything
even my once luminous dreams,
the man waving the gun above his head
says as if reciting a poem
to an audience of Martians.
He did say we were overrun
by Martians before he issued
his threat to the street corner
of bad-luck morning pedestrians
now frozen in their tracks.
If anyone moves you will meet
your Maker before your time,
he warns eloquently and thinks,
On Mars, of course, no one dies
no one is ignored or despised
no one goes hungry or is lonely.

The tactical unit's sharpshooter
who yesterday had taken his young son
to a film about space travel
landing on another planet, not Mars,
has the frenzied man in his sights.

The sharpshooter's wife, truth be known,
is having an affair with a weaponless poet
and when the sharpshooter finds out
in week or two, as he certainly will,
creating, of course, another perilous situation
and another sad news story.

The poet, amazingly, it should be revealed,
wrote two anguished lines a year ago resembling
Darkness obscures everything
even my once luminous dreams—
such is sometimes the way of the world
and it is a small mystifying world, after all.

Gluxoxgluxoxgluxoxgluxoxgluxox

I was at an intersection of historic proportions
(it had appeared in three sci-fi novels I had read
at three different times in my all-too-earthbound life)
when the all-too-human-looking female robot
leaned in my car window
and I thought I'd seen this in a hundred films.
Expecting a clichéd proposition such as
You want a date, sweetie?
or, You in the mood for a good time?
Instead she utters with automated sensuality
Gluxoxgluxoxgluxoxgluxoxgluxox
and I think, What intersection am I really at?
Where in time and space?
I don't recall time travelling recently
but here is the most beautiful all-too-human-looking
female robot repeatedly uttering
Gluxoxgluxoxgluxoxgluxoxgluxox
Gluxoxgluxoxgluxoxgluxoxgluxox
Gluxoxgluxoxgluxoxgluxoxgluxox ...
I have no idea what to say
something lustful or erudite
and she says, *Erudition isn't called for tonight,*
as if she had read my mind
suddenly I realize maybe it is her poem
I want to voice authorial protest
to take command of my thoughts
instead the automatic sensuality of
Gluxoxgluxoxgluxoxgluxoxgluxox
Gluxoxgluxoxgluxoxgluxoxgluxox
Gluxoxgluxoxgluxoxgluxoxgluxox ...
I take out my wallet

offer everything I have
to leave me alone
and just then she smiles
and I see teeth
a colour I could not describe
my car turning into something else
a small futuristic spaceship of sorts
and I fear I will be rearranged next
it is, after all, her poem
this all-too-human-looking female robot
and all I can do is go along for the ride.

You Look the Endangered Animal in the Eye

There, blocking your path,
despite all former definitions
and a lifetime of visits to zoos
in out-of-the-way locales
is a difficult to define
endangered animal
a creature larger than all your
fears and failures combined.

On another level (less likely)
unruly yet not unreal
you look the endangered animal in the eye
detect not only the deviance and strategy
but all the plots and blueprints for pain
and sidestep agilely
save the essential aspects of self
maintain the need for memory and love.

On a more direct level (more likely)
courteous yet overly real
you look the endangered animal in the eye
it is the wrong eye and you get sideswiped
damaging memory and love
leaving you crying for an altered landscape
where distance is irrelevant
and no one squints to throw you off guard.

You pray for a revelation
a revelation showing a path
around or past the endangered animal
so next time you have a way out.

Coastal City. Tourist Season. The Apocalypse.

Shimmering sky canopying a mystical day
every imaginable colour of a fantastical rainbow
baffling denizens and tourists alike
in the heart of downtown during tourist season.

What number cruise ship is this?
a smiling accountant of souls
asks you as you rush to the library
to return ten overdue poetry books
and an annotated bible with as many typos
as in your typo-punctuated, typo-punctured life.
Later, wandering the stacks, among spirited books,
you hear a professor of dark demographics say,
Absurdity is heightened in tourist season, you know.
I don't know, you say, arguing in whispers
that absurdity is an equal-season reality
not that reality and tourist season
should be whispered in the same breath
but metaphysics is better in spring or fall
not tourist season, but you've been wrong before.
Relentless time and rickety time machines,
a scientist tells you as you start to leave,
then a nearby theologian inquires,
Where do you go from here, nearly lost soul?
Nowhere and everywhere, you declare,
and both the scientist and the theologian laugh
as if laughter was going out of style.
Outside, more human interaction
is about to occur, excitement and trepidation
arm-in-arm like bewildered lovers.
A cheerful politician of stability stumbles

at your feet, campaign promises
bleeding lavishly over the sidewalk
asking for your electoral support.
I'll vote for your doppelgänger
next election, not you, you whisper
library-soft again, yelling will come later
as eloquent as tourist season will allow—
what's next on the human struggle agenda?
A beautician of the inner and outer selves
asks you if you desire the full treatment,
a complete toe-to-cranium makeover,
deep discount today because of the shimmering sky.
No thanks, you say, you're used to your deformities
and less than consequential aspects,
but maybe, you add, *we should ask the droll scientists*
and amusing theologians if they'd like your treatment.
Hell is boredom, boredom is hell,
you figure it out, bystander,
a busker sings as you approach.
A few tottering steps away,
a half-dead poet or half-alive poseur
who's checking credentials today
recites someone else's unhinged poem:
Count the beans of existence
exist in a galaxy of dreams
fall headlong and disillusioned
into forgetfulness ...
Shaking your head, you sidestep a lawyer
defending the human spirit
smiling at the billable hours
teeth whiter than last winter's
record-breaking snowstorm,
you wonder who you'll see next, friend or foe.
An entrepreneurial pornographer offers you glossy photos
high-definition videos, and lifelike souvenirs of decadence,

you name it, and you take a peek, give a touch, get mildly aroused,
but claim the end is nigh, the shimmering sky, after all,
and you have no time for bits of depravity so late in the day.
So you walk down to the harbour
study the behemoth of a cruise ship—
What number cruise ship is this?
you recall someone else's words—
as the passengers re-board
and an exceedingly tall couple
perfectly misshapen and magnificently malformed
catches your beyond-exhausted eye.
Aliens, surely aliens,
you yell, and they turn
give you the space-age evil eye
as you await the end of the world
or the beginning of autumn,
whichever comes first.

Your Doppelgänger's Afterlife Dreams: A Theatre-of-the-Absurd Prayer/Poem

The dead of another night
your doppelgänger's wretched sleep
of tossing and turning
waking you a hundred disorienting times
your doppelgänger an afterlife dreamer
poorly performed Theatre-of-the-Absurd sleep
a prayer aspiring to be a poem
you caught in the grip of an illogical word

afterlife / life after
            get your contrary ducks
            and elusive metaphors
         . all in an orderly row
all the circuitous thoughts
all the proofs, neat or messy,
            of death
            and near-death
            words stolen and broken
            sentenced to life
            rearranged into death sentences
such are dreams
            imagination
            nightmares
            subconscious flights of fancy
            jumping off miraculous cliffs
                  language means nothing
                  hitting the bottom
            everything as you fall
            as heavy as Sisyphus's rock
            without documents

　　　　　　　　or money-saving coupons
　　　　　　　　or get-out-of-jail-free cards
　　　　　　　　or farewell concert-of-the-year tickets
　　　　brace yourself for the silence
　　　　prepare yourself for the unimagined
　　　　make your prayer succinct yet potent
　　　　　　　　you've prayed before
　　　　　　　　not these high stakes
　　　　　　　　like betting on eternity
　　　　　　　　double or nothing
　　the end of time
　　　　　　a time of endings
　　　　　　why did you sleep through
　　　　　　the end of the movie?
　　　　　　perforating the word *endless*
　　　　　　praying as if there's no tomorrow
　　optimist turned pessimist
　　　　　　in mid flight
　　　　　　abducted by space aliens
　　　　　　disguised as talk-show hosts
　　　　　　with perilous senses of humour
　　　　　　like our worst joke-tellers
　　　　　　stutterers of the absurd
　　　　　　brokenhearted absurdity
　　　　　　looking for new careers
　　　　　　and a stronger cup of coffee
　　　　　　caffeinated epiphanies
　　refusing to jump just now
　　　　　　starting to dance
　　　　　　choreographed or improvised
　　　　　　little choice this time around
　　　　　　what had you been studying
　　　　　　stumbling through time
　　　　　　looking down
　　　　　　clarity or vagueness

seeing a program from the first performance
of *Waiting for Godot*
you dreamed you were there
the best seat in the house
wearing a bow tie and fancy suspenders
the colour of madness
remind yourself: language means everything
as you assume flight
the glorious optimism of flight
higher than the heavens
now the descent turns to ascent
before the end of this prayer
disguised as a poem
disguised as a life …

The End of the World

And when the world does end
as it surely will, place your bets,
either in cataclysm or listlessness
I wonder who will hit the final home run
in the bottom of the ninth
or score the last memorable goal
in an exciting championship game
or who will sink the final free throw
in a schoolyard game
where winning isn't everything
who will write the final poem
in ink or blood or dancing electrons
last painting or nearly last
a few more brushstrokes
almost capturing the beauty of sanctity
last story, last novel, last kick at the can
sing the final song
off key or mellifluously
and at the end
what inspiration will there be?

All those obits left unwritten
all those apologies left dangling in the air
and desperate prayers not quite right or finished
all those acts of contrition unperformed
pleas for forgiveness unarticulated
not enough time
never enough time
especially at world's end.

I want a poem with a good ending
all the thoughts and uncertainties
and missed opportunities
tied together with metaphoric hope
even if that poem is about
the end of the world
preposterous and ludicrous
as it might be.

Acknowledgements

The author acknowledges with gratitude that some of the poems, sometimes in earlier versions, in this collection have appeared in the following publications: *Abstract Magazine* (online) (US), *Adanna Literary Journal* (US), *Amsterdam Quarterly* (online) / *Amsterdam Quarterly* 2015 Yearbook (Netherlands), *audience* (US), *Bard* (UK), *Belleville Park Pages* (France & UK), *Bête Noire* (US), *Calamario* (US), *carte blanche* (online) (Canada), *Channel* (Ireland), *Eye to the Telescope* (online) (US), *The Fieldstone Review* (online) (Canada), *Forge* (US), *Grain* (Canada), *Grey Borders Magazine* (Canada), *Helios Quarterly Magazine* (US), *The Helix* (US), *Illumen* (US), *The Impressment Gang* (Canada), *Inclement* (UK), *Jones Av.* (Canada), *The Laughing Dog* (US), *mgversion2>datura* (France), *Nebo: A Literary Journal* (US), *Night Picnic Journal* (US), *The Ogham Stone* (Ireland), *Ottawa Arts Review* (Canada), *Outposts of Beyond* (US), *Penny Ante Review* (US), *Phantom Drift: A Journal of New Fabulism* (US), *The Poetry Bus* (Ireland), *Poetry Quarterly* (US), *Polar Borealis Magazine* (digital) (Canada), *Prole* (UK), *The Rampallian* (US), *Revival* (Ireland), *San Pedro River Review* (US), *Sisyphus Quarterly* (US), *Songs of Eretz Poetry E-zine* (US), *Star*Line* (US), *Tales from the Moonlit Path* (online) (US), *Tigershark Magazine* (digital) (UK), *Tipton Poetry Journal* (US), *Tower Poetry* (Canada), *Trysts of Fate* (US), *The Wild Word* (online) (Germany), *[Word]: A Journal of Canadian Poetry, Write* (Canada), and *The Writers' Café Magazine* (online) (UK); in the anthologies *Alternative Apocalypse* (Edited by Debora Godfrey and Bob Brown, B Cubed Press, Kiona, WA, 2019), *The Furious Gazelle Presents: Halloween* (Edited by Tess Tabak and E. Kirshe, *The Furious Gazelle*, Coppell, TX, 2021), and *Lost and Found: Tales of Things Gone Missing* (Edited by Terri Karsten, Wagonbridge Publishing, Winona, MN, 2019); in the chapbooks *A Fanciful Geography* (erbacce-press, Liverpool, UK, 2010) by J. J. Steinfeld, and *Open Heart 2, Anthology of Canadian Poetry* (Selected by John B. Lee, Beret Days Press, Toronto, ON, 2008).

The author wishes to thank all the editors involved with these publications.

About the Author

Poet, fiction writer, and playwright J. J. Steinfeld was born in a Displaced Persons Camp in Germany, of Polish Jewish Holocaust survivor parents. After receiving his master's degree in history from Trent University and spending two years in a PhD program at the University of Ottawa, he abandoned that program and moved in 1980 to Prince Edward Island to write full time. Steinfeld lives in Charlottetown, where he is patiently waiting for Godot's arrival and a phone call from Kafka. While waiting, he has published twenty-two books: two novels, *Our Hero in the Cradle of Confederation* (1987) and *Word Burials* (2009), thirteen short story collections—*The Apostate's Tattoo* (1983), *Forms of Captivity and Escape* (1988), *Unmapped Dreams* (1989), *The Miraculous Hand and Other Stories* (1991), *Dancing at the Club Holocaust* (1993), *Disturbing Identities* (1997), *Should the Word Hell Be Capitalized?* (1999), *Anton Chekhov Was Never in Charlottetown* (2000), *Would You Hide Me?* (2003), *A Glass Shard and Memory* (2010), *Madhouses in Heaven, Castles in Hell* (2015), *An Unauthorized Biography of Being* (2016), and *Gregor Samsa Was Never in The Beatles* (2019)—and seven poetry collections, *An Affection for Precipices* (2006), *Misshapenness* (2009), *Identity Dreams and Memory Sounds* (2014), *Absurdity, Woe Is Me, Glory Be* (2017), *A Visit to the Kafka Café* (2018), *Morning Bafflement and Timeless Puzzlement* (2020), and *Somewhat Absurd, Somehow Existential* (2021), along with two short-fiction chapbooks, *Curiosity to Satisfy and Fear to Placate* (2003) and *Not a Second More, Not a Second Less* (2005), and three poetry chapbooks, *Existence Is a Hoax, a Woman in Fishnet Stockings Told Me When I Was Twenty* (2003), *Where War Finds You* (2008), and *A Fanciful Geography* (2010). From 1981, when Steinfeld published his first short story, to 1986, when his first one-act play was produced, and 2001, when he published his first poem, to the publication of his 2021 Guernica Editions poetry collection, *Somewhat Absurd, Somehow Existential,* nearly 500 of his short stories and more than 1000 poems have appeared in anthologies and periodicals, in Canada and with at least one piece internationally in twenty countries, and over 60 of his one-act plays and a handful of full-length plays have been performed in Canada and the United States. In 2017, Guernica Editions published both a poetry collection by Steinfeld in their Essential Poets Series, *Absurdity, Woe Is Me, Glory Be*, and also a book in their Essential Writers Series, *J. J. Steinfeld: Essays on His Works*, compiled and edited by Sandra Singer, which took a critical look at the author's extensive and prolific writings of poetry, fiction, and plays.